MAIN
CHILDREN'S
ROOM

D1497596

DISCARD
FROM THE
COLLECTION

CITY OF
OAKLAND

OAKLAND PUBLIC LIBRARY
OAKLAND, CA

Children's Room
Oakland Public Library
125 - 14th Street
Oakland, CA 94612
(510) 238-3615

MAIN
CHILDREN'S
ROOM

Felicia Bond

Poinsettia
and the
Firefighters

LAURA GERINGER BOOKS
An Imprint of HarperCollins*Publishers*

Poinsettia and the Firefighters
Copyright © 1984 by Felicia Bond
Printed in the U.S.A. All rights reserved.
www.harperchildrens.com

Library of Congress Cataloging-in-Publication Data
Bond, Felicia
    Poinsettia and the firefighters / Felicia Bond
    p. cm.
"Laura Geringer Books"
    Summary: Poinsettia the Pig feels lonely and afraid of the dark until she learns
that there is someone else awake and keeping watch all night: the firefighters.
    ISBN 0-06-053509-1. — ISBN 0-06-053510-5 (lib. bdg.).
    [1. Night—Fiction. 2. Fear—Fiction. 3. Fire fighters—Fiction. 4. Pigs—Fiction].
I. Title.
PZ7.B63666Pp 2003   83-46169
[E]—dc21   CIP
                                                                                        AC

1 2 3 4 5 6 7 8 9 10

New Edition 2003

OCT 2 0 2003

MAIN
CHILDREN'S
ROOM

2467 2556

To 132 Pondfield Road West

One Saturday morning Poinsettia's father said, "Poinsettia, how would you like to have your own room? I fixed up the two rooms on the top floor, one just for you, and one just for Petunia."

Poinsettia could hardly believe her ears. That afternoon Julius and Pierre moved into her old room.

"I bet you'll be scared to sleep by yourself," Pierre snorted.

"I bet I won't," Poinsettia said.

"You can have my favorite night-light," offered Chick Pea.

"No," Poinsettia grunted. "Only babies sleep with night-lights."

Poinsettia loved her new room. She admired it
all evening and into the night.

Finally her father had to call up the stairs. "Turn out your light, Poinsettia," he said. "It's way past your bedtime."

"I can't even see my hoof in front of my face," Poinsettia thought.

She opened the curtains, but there was no
moonlight or starlight. One by one the neighbors'
lights went out.

Poinsettia's mother and father turned off their light too. The night was very dark.

Suddenly something went CLANK!

"Petunia!" Poinsettia shouted.

"That was only your radiator," mumbled Petunia.

"I didn't see a radiator," Poinsettia said. "Are you sure I have one?" CLANK! went the sound.

"Let's invent a secret code," Poinsettia said. "If we hear a scary noise, I'll say 'peep' to make sure you're awake. Then you tell me what the noise is, okay?"

"Okay," said Petunia.

Poinsettia went back to bed.

Something creaked, v-e-r-y slowly. "Peep!" said
Poinsettia.

"The stairs," said Petunia.

Something scratched, v-e-r-y roughly. "Peep!"
said Poinsettia.

"A branch," said Petunia.

Something thumped, very loudly. "Peep!" said
Poinsettia. "Peep! Peep! . . . PEEP!"

Petunia was asleep.

"Oh, no!" Poinsettia whispered. "I am the only
one awake."

She thought about the thump and the dark places where it might be.

The thump came again, and it seemed louder and closer than before. Poinsettia closed her eyes. "Please let it be morning," she wished.

When she opened her eyes, there was a light outside.

It was pink and gold.

"The sun!" Poinsettia said.

The light got bigger and brighter. But it was not sunrise.

It was a fire on the telephone wire in front of
Poinsettia's house.

"MOM!" Poinsettia shouted. "MOM! DAD!"

Poinsettia's mother called the fire department,

and the entire family watched the firefighters put out the flames.

Afterward, three of the firefighters came into the house and filled out their report.

"You have a keen eye," one of them said to Poinsettia.

"Did the alarm wake you up?" Poinsettia asked.

"Oh, no," said the firefighter. "I'm the night watchman. I stay awake all night."

"I'm a night watcher too," Poinsettia said.

The firefighters waved good-bye.

Poinsettia went back to her room and looked out the window. The night was still dark.

Then Poinsettia saw it was not quite as dark as before.

Shining through the trees was the light from the fire station six blocks away.

"I am not the only one awake," Poinsettia said.

There were more noises that night, but they didn't bother Poinsettia.

SQUEAK

DRIP

CLATTER

And when the sun finally rose . . .

Poinsettia was not awake to see it.